MILES LEDOUX

GOOD WITCH, BAD WITCH

Winter in Veil, Book 2

First published by ABCs 2025

This novel is entirely a work of fiction. The names, characters, and incidents portrayed in it are the work of the author's imagination. Any resemblance to actual persons, living or dead, events, or localities is entirely coincidental.

First edition

ISBN: 978-1-882508-82-2

Cover art by Rachel Kelli
Editing by Julie Mianecki

This book was professionally typeset on Reedsy.
Find out more at reedsy.com

Preface

Ev'ry night when I go out
The monkey's on the table
Take a stick and knock it off
Pop! goes the weasel

Prologue

Steam rose from the witch's concoction. She gave it a sniff…and let out a sigh of contentment. She'd gotten it just right.

She glanced at the clock. Just seconds to midnight. The time had come.

She set the steaming mug of tea beside her printer and clicked her computer mouse. Her computer's tiny camera activated and a small, rectangular image of herself appeared on the screen. She gave the camera a brilliant smile. "Hello, my beautiful viewers! Candy Apples here, and welcome back to my channel! It's Friday night, midnight, so once again I'm live-streaming, answering your questions about Paganism in my ongoing effort to promote awareness and understanding, and debunk the many, many myths about this spiritual path. If you're a first-time viewer, my name is Candy, I'm nineteen years old, and I'm a Celtic Wiccan and neo-Pagan. If you don't know what those words mean—and trust me, you probably don't, even if you think you do—I have a video explaining it, to which you can click the link below. Now, you know the drill: type in your questions, and if I have an answer, I'll tell you."

She paused to sip her tea. The questions and various greetings were already rolling in, but she kept her own pace rather than hurry to keep up with them. If someone had a question they urgently wanted answered, they could ask again.

"Okay," she said, "here's a question I've kind of answered before: 'As a Pagan, is Halloween your Christmas?' I talk about this in my video on winter solstice holidays around the world, and also in my video about the Wheel of the Year. Halloween is *not* our Christmas; Halloween is our Halloween. It's an important holiday, but not necessarily the *most* important. Some consider it the Wiccan new year. The Pagan name for it is Samhain, and we usually celebrate it with a ritual—though most years, many of us have plans for October thirty-first, so we hold the ritual sometime before. Our winter solstice holiday is called Yule—maybe you've heard of the *yule* log? Different Wiccans have different favorite holidays, just as some of you might prefer the Easter Bunny over Santa Claus."

She took another sip and scanned the incoming questions, though in truth she'd already spotted the next one she wanted to answer. She spoke as if she were reading it for the first time: "'My friend says there's no such thing as witches because magic isn't real.' First of all, not all witches use magic. Choice of spiritual practice is up to the individual. Second, I don't believe in the Christian god, but I wouldn't go around saying that Christians don't exist, because that would be kinda silly. And so is your friend."

She scanned some more. Her eyes landed on, *Hav u ever ben in a orjy? If u say no, ur lyin.*

"Aaand we have our first troll of the night!" she announced, clicking rapidly. "And—he's blocked. And reported. Hopefully we'll get through tonight without any death threats," she added cheerfully.

Thus it went on for several minutes. Many questions required only simple answers, often in the negative. *Do you sacrifice animals?* "No." *Do you have a "dark Bible"?* "No." *Aren't Wicca* and witchcraft the same thing? "Nope." *Do you sleep with goats?* "Ew." *Why do you prefer an alternative lifestyle?* "To me, that's called Christianity."

Then Candy sighed and, after a moment's hesitation, said, "Here's one that's probably another troll, but I'm going to answer it anyway. 'Why don't you love Jesus?' So...like Jesus, I try to strive for unconditional love for all living things. But for me, Jesus isn't a symbol of divinity or faith. I've got others. The person asking this question probably feels threatened because I'm comfortable in a faith that doesn't see Jesus as the be-all and end-all of religion. And..." She paused. She wanted to word this just right. "This...this question is more a reflection on the questioner. My impression is that they dismiss and/or vilify religions other than their own, and so they assume that everyone—every other religious group—does the same. And that's just not true, at least not in my case. I don't believe in Christian practices like Lent or Communion, and some of them might seem strange or unhealthy to me, but even that doesn't give me license to call all Christians what a lot of people call us—creepy, or whack-jobs. They see us following a different spiritual practice and they see it as a challenge to theirs, which it's not. I don't see us developing a mutual respect anytime soon, but somehow we all have to learn to co-exist." She needed a large gulp of tea after that.

Searching for a less loaded question, she landed on, *I want to go to a Wiccan ceremony, but I'm worried they'll want me to do sexual things.*

"Oh, honey!" she burst out, forgetting to read the question aloud. "You don't have to do *anything* you're not comfortable with, and definitely nothing like that! Sex isn't compulsory in Wicca, no matter what you've heard. We're all about respecting boundaries. And…and if it'll make you feel better, I've been practicing Wicca for four years, and I'm still a virgin. I've never been intimate with anyone." *Not consensually, anyway,* she thought.

The next question was, *Do Wiccan witches use wands like in Harry Potter?* "Well," said Candy, "actually yes, some of us do, but it's not the only tool we use. Like, mine is an elemental wand—here, I'll show you." She stretched her hand out toward the nearby altar.

With her attention on the wand that was just out of reach, she didn't see the change that came over the rolling comment section. The questions and general remarks all but disappeared, replaced by a slew of statements very similar to one another:

Behind u!

Behind You

Omg behind you

LOOK BEHIND YOU!!!!

Wand in hand, Candy turned back to the computer. Her eyes went to the tiny screen showing herself and the open doorway behind her…

She screamed.

I

Violet woke up with a start. It was dark. Something was making a noise—something right beside her! She needed light, needed to see, but she'd never slept in this room before, didn't know where the light switch was— wait—yes, she did! There was a lamp at the head of her bed. She reached up and turned it on.

The room was empty; there was no danger. Rain pattered on the window, accounting for the noise. Violet sank back onto the pillow, feeling her heart pounding.

Violet. That was her name now. Whatever her true name was had been lost with all her other memories of her past and her identity, right up until yesterday morning. Briefly, she cast her mind back across the events of the previous day—waking up injured, frightened, and confused; trying to retrieve her memory; being taken in by her new friends, Cyanne Grogan and her mother, Jen. This was a spare bedroom in their three-story house out in the country.

Violet tilted her head back to regard the lamp. She couldn't recall having taken notice of it last night, but she must have. That's how she'd known it was there, even though she couldn't see it. That had been yesterday's other great discovery: in spite of her amnesia, she retained a perfect memory of everything she saw and did. It was bizarre, and she was not yet used to it.

She reached up to turn the lamp off again but hesitated, then let her hand drop. Last night she'd been too tired to pay close attention to her surroundings; now, taking them in, becoming aware of what was around her, seemed to calm her down. The room was done in lavender wallpaper. On the ceiling was a large, circular glass light, probably operated by the switch over beside the door. There was a closet, an empty bookcase, a cedar chest, and some cardboard boxes piled in the corner with the name *Azura* written on one of them. That was the name of Cy's sister, the one doing an internship in Antarctica. Perhaps this was intended to be her room when she returned.

Violet took a deep breath and let it out slowly. Her heart had stopped pounding, but now she felt restless. She swung her legs over the side of the bed and slid her feet into the slippers Cy had left for her. Wrapping herself in the bed's top blanket, she eased open the door and stepped out into the hall.

Just outside her door, on one side, was the staircase. As it went up, it doubled back on itself; going down, it went straight to the first floor. On the other side, the corridor narrowed, leading to more bedrooms and a second staircase that led only down.

This was a large house.

Violet noticed a light on in one of the rooms ahead. She padded her way over and looked in.

Cy was there, sitting on her bed in her pajamas with the calico cat Roswell purring in her lap. She looked up. "Can't sleep?"

Violet gave a wan smile and shook her head. She cast a glance around Cy's room. To her surprise, it was almost as bare as the one she'd just left.

Cy seemed to guess her thoughts. "I never finished unpacking after we moved here," she said. "Guess I've been putting it off out of bitterness."

Rain and wind slammed wildly against the window. "We were almost caught in that," Cy murmured.

Violet shivered and pulled the blanket closer around her.

"Rob called me again," Cy went on. "I threatened to tell Mom about him. Maybe I should anyway."

Violet remembered Cy's ex-boyfriend, who had tried to extort favors from the teenage girl, then assaulted her when she refused. Violet had happened to be nearby, and intervened. Then Cy had helped Violet when she collapsed from exhaustion due to her injuries (though what had precipitated those injuries she had no idea). That was how they'd met.

"What about you?" asked Cy. "What's keeping you up?"

Violet shrugged. "I was hoping some sleep might get my memories back. They might be gone forever." She paused. "I'm not ready to accept that."

Cy nodded. "All right. This calls for emergency protocols. Follow me." She led Violet down the back staircase, which curved at the bottom, leading into the kitchen. Five minutes later, the two of them sat at the corner of a long wooden table positioned below a large set of windows, sharing a bowl of strawberries, which they dipped in whipped cream. The kitchen looked old-fashioned, with wooden paneling and countertops, and a brick flue over the stove in the corner. Wind rattled the back door beside them.

"So," said Cy, "yesterday we started making a list of things we found out about you."

"Yeah," said Violet, "but all that really helped us figure out is that I have a good memory. I might know all the words to a song, but that doesn't necessarily mean I *like* the song, or that it has anything to do with me at all."

"Well, then let's find out. We can have you listen to the radio, find out what kind of music you like. I bet there's a ton of stuff we can still discover about you. We can find out your favorite food, find out if you're gay, straight, bi, ace, or whatever, we can find out what religion you ascribe to, if any—like, do you believe in God?"

Violet raised an eyebrow. "Uh...maybe...not?"

"Okay, so maybe you're an atheist, like me. We can also find out—hey, I know!" Getting up, Cy grabbed the food and led Violet into the next room, a den with a sofa curved around a TV. Cy set the food down on a coffee table and started pulling DVDs off the shelves. "We can find out what sort of movies you like," she explained. "That okay with you?"

"Sure," replied Violet, settling on the sofa.

A DVD pile started growing beside Cy, including *Memento*, *Overboard*, *50 First Dates*, *Paycheck*, and *The Bourne Identity*.

"As long as they don't involve amnesia. I don't want to think about that right now."

Cy froze in place with the movie *Total Recall* in her hand. "Um...you know what? I have an even better idea." She shoved the DVDs back on the shelves.

* * *

The rain had stopped by the time Jen came down for breakfast, dressed in her sheriff's deputy's uniform. When she couldn't find any strawberries, she looked into the den and found it occupied by two figures just beginning to stir from sleep, one huddled under a blanket on the sofa, the other in an armchair, wrapped in Jen's overcoat from the hall closet. "Good morning," said Jen with some amusement. She noticed the strawberries, whipped cream, and a board game on the coffee table. "Slumber party?"

Cy rubbed sleep from her eyes and grumbled something that sounded like, "Appetune tuss."

"Aptitude test?" Jen interpreted. She noted that the board game was *Trivial Pursuits*.

"I did okay with popular culture," Violet commented groggily.

"But she sucks at sports and leisure," said Cy. "She knows rules and stuff but not stats or historical figures."

"I see," said Jen. She sat on the arm of the sofa. "Nelly, the station called. I'm afraid they weren't able to trace the clothing you were wearing; it was too generic. We showed a headshot of you around at the bed and breakfast and the nearest motel, but no one recognized you. I'm sorry."

"She's actually going by Violet now," Cy told her.

Jen looked from Cy to her guest in surprise. "Violet?"

Violet nodded.

Jen stared at her for a moment, her mouth parted, and in her eyes Violet was startled to see something resembling...horror? Grief? Anguish? In the next moment, whatever it was had disappeared. If not for her gift, Violet might have thought she'd imagined it.

"Well...Violet...I also have to tell you they haven't found anything substantive at the old highway where you first woke up."

"Maybe we should put an ad in the paper with your picture," Cy suggested. "We could put it online, too."

"That's the other thing," said Jen. "The *Veil Chronicle* wants to see you."

"I want to do the fingerprinting as soon as possible," Violet interjected.

"Good idea. When you're ready, come on down to the station. The *Chronicle* isn't too far from there."

Violet decided to take a shower while Cy ate breakfast. Before getting in, she peeled off the bandage from her forehead, exposing the grisly head wound that had likely brought about her amnesia. It was scabbing over but still felt quite tender.

After Cy had finished her turn in the shower, she found Violet staring at the mirror in the downstairs bathroom, attempting to hide the wound somehow with her hair, and having little success. Before Violet knew what was happening, Cy's hands slid a woolen beanie over her head from behind. "How's that?"

The wound was completely hidden. "I'll take it," said Violet.

As they started to put on their jackets and shoes, a thought occurred to Violet. "Wait a minute. If your mom's already left, how are we getting to town?"

"Well, we're about to find out if an old adage is true."

Not long after, they were cruising along the road on a pair of bicycles. Violet reveled in the scent of autumn, the colors of leaves streaming past on either side. These bikes, Cy had explained, belonged to her mother and sister, as her own was still back at Riverbend Park, where they'd first met.

The fingerprinting didn't last long. The sheriff was away from the station, but a few of the deputies offered Cy and Violet congratulations on their accomplishments yesterday. Thanks to the two of them, a missing girl had been found and a kidnapper had been apprehended. One deputy asked Cy when she was going to become a law officer like her mother. Cy laughed half-heartedly.

The building that housed the *Chronicle* offices was only a block away. They left the bikes at the sheriff's station and walked. On a Saturday morning, Veil's Main Street was quiet, with very little traffic to speak of, auto or pedestrian. One vehicle that did catch Violet's attention was a car the same color as her name, parked outside the offices of the *Chronicle*.

Violet was nervous about the newspaper staff asking her questions, particularly since she felt like she didn't have any answers. However, the editor treated her kindly and said they just wanted an account of what she and Cy did yesterday. Cy told her they wanted to put an ad out to see if they could find anyone who might know Violet. The editor took Violet's picture and said she'd take care of it while the two young women gave their interview.

The interview was conducted by a reporter named Kelly Upshaw. She was in her late forties, stout, and had short, curly brown hair. As she asked questions, she took notes with a bright red pen. "So, Deputy Grogan then led the three of you back to town?"

"Well," said Cy, "she would've, but she, um, dropped her GPS and it got broken, so she was gonna have us spend the night in the ranger station. She was afraid that if we tried to find our way back, we'd get lost and stuck out there with no shelter."

"But, according to the sheriff's report, Deputy Grogan led you out of the woods and onto Mountain Boulevard when the rest of you didn't know which direction the town was in." In saying this, she laid down the pen and picked up a different set of notes to check.

"That was only at the end," said Cy. "It was Violet who led us most of the way back. She has a perfect memory. She remembers everything she sees—except the stuff she doesn't remember, from before her injury—so even though she'd only been through the forest once before, she could lead us exactly the way she came—why aren't you writing any of this down?"

Kelly had picked up another pen, lime green this time, but was merely holding it, resting the end against her chin. "I'm focusing more on the rescue and less on the…amnesia aspect," she said, failing to mask the skepticism in her tone.

Cy's brow furrowed. "Are you saying you don't believe her?" She glanced at Violet, but Violet's attention was distracted by what appeared to be an argument across the room, between the editor and a striking young woman with strawberry blond hair.

"It isn't a matter of what *I* believe," replied Kelly, "but what our readers will believe. If we can't provide evidence of an extraordinary claim—"

"Evidence? You want evidence? You can test her memory right now. She could turn her back and you can change one thing on your desk, and she'll pick it out. Hell, you could change one thing in this whole room and she'd—"

"Cy, Cy, it's all right," Violet assured her. As Cy scowled in annoyance, Violet asked Kelly, "Did you have any more questions?"

Kelly regarded her appraisingly, as if tempted to take up Cy on her offer. "No, that's all," she said. "Thank you."

Cy was still irate as they exited the building. "The most interesting thing that could possibly happen in this town, and they're not gonna report about it?! This is stupid. *You're* the one who saved us."

"Cy, it's okay," said Violet. "Remember, I didn't believe it either, at first. It's no big deal."

"She barely even asked us about how we unmasked the kidnapper!" Cy ranted.

"Well, it *was* kind of guesswork on our part."

Cy sighed. "I'm sorry, it's just that I expected Rob to be in there—this is where he works—and I had this whole tirade prepared for when he tried to talk to me. But I didn't even see him."

"You mean Rob Mulroy?" said a voice.

They turned to see the young woman with strawberry blond hair, who had just come out behind them.

"Yeah," said Cy. "He's my ex."

The woman pursed her lips and nodded. "I met him last time I was here. He said he'd get the editor to take me seriously if I, ahem, 'dated' him."

Cy threw up her hands. "Has he even *tried* not being a jerk?"

Grinning, the woman held out her hand. "I'm Candy."

"Cyanne. This is Violet."

Violet had been staring at Candy, a slight rosiness building in her cheeks. When Candy offered her hand, she blinked hard, as if coming out of a trance. "Hi," she said softly as they shook hands. Then, clearing her throat, she asked, "So, what weren't they taking seriously about you?"

Candy sighed. "It's not just them, unfortunately. It's the majority of the town. Here." She gave each of them a business card with a headshot, the name *Candy Apples*, and a YouTube link. "I'm uploading a new video tonight explaining it all. You can find out all about it. Nice meeting you guys!" With that, she skipped down the steps, her hair bouncing.

Violet's eyes followed her. Then she became aware of Cy eyeing her with amusement, and her blush deepened.

"Do you want to go after her and get her number?" Cy asked.

"Will you keep your voice down?" Violet hissed.

Then she frowned.

Candy was headed straight for the purple car she'd noticed earlier. She was unlocking it, reaching for the door handle.

"Wait—wait!!"

Cy watched, bewildered, as Violet bolted down the steps. "Wait, don't—"

Candy opened the door a moment before Violet plowed into her, knocking her over. In the next instant, with a loud *pop*, a gallon of blood geysered out of the car through the open door, cascading over the spot where Candy had been standing.

Cy covered her mouth with both hands.

Violet rolled off Candy, who stared at the blood in horror.

II

"It's not blood," said Deputy Derrick. "It's cherry soda. There's still some in the pump." He pointed at the device sitting on the driver's seat, which looked like a miniature confetti cannon with extra tubing attached.

"Well, that's good, isn't it?" said Cy, standing to the side with Candy and Violet. "It should be easy for you to trace who bought a lot of that recently."

Derrick shot her a glower. Violet remembered that this was the deputy—the only one—who'd looked unhappy yesterday when Jen Grogan restored the missing girl to her parents. Just what was his issue with the senior deputy?

"Interesting," Candy murmured.

"What?" asked Violet.

"Well, I'm allergic to cherries. But the flavor in cherry soda is artificial. Is it a coincidence, or was he trying to make me have a reaction? In which case, how is he smart enough to rig that machine, but dumb enough—"

"Miss Windom," the deputy interrupted her sharply, "I spent almost eight hours yesterday on my feet, looking for a missing kid. Then, around one in the morning, I had to get out of bed— because it was all hands on deck yesterday and they had to wake up *someone*—and investigate your supposed home invasion,

15

which was somehow quiet enough for your mother to sleep through. I'm tired and impatient, so I'm going to be blunt: wasting the time of law enforcement is a punishable crime and we will charge you if you keep this up."

Cy was about to shout in outrage, but Candy raised a hand and said, in as even a voice as possible, "I'm not making this up, Deputy. I'm not...fabricating these attacks. This is the fourth time—"

"Enough," Derrick snapped. "Miss Windom, I went over your home last night. There was no sign of forced entry. No one broke in and attacked you."

"I have six hundred witnesses." Seeing the looks Cy and Violet gave her, she explained, "I was live-streaming."

"Yes, I watched your video," said Derrick. "All your viewers saw was a shadow. There was no attacker. You faked it."

Candy looked away. Her expression was wooden, but her eyes shone with unshed tears.

"I can vouch for her," said Violet, her voice tinged with anger. Derrick rolled his eyes as she went on, "I saw her car as we went in the building, and Candy was already inside. When she came out just after us, she went right to her car. She couldn't have rigged the—whatever it is."

Derrick shut the car door and pointed to the window. "You couldn't have seen that the device wasn't in the car the first time you looked."

"No, but the second time, I saw that some items in the car had been moved around, like that bag and her sunglasses. I thought someone was hiding in the car, about to attack her."

"Items moved around," Derrick repeated, deadpan.

"Violet has a perfect memory!" Cy reminded him. "Seriously, how is no one getting this?"

16

"Wait, really?" Candy sounded impressed.

"Okay, look," said Derrick, "if you really want us to investigate, then we'll have to take your car and everything in it as evidence." He waited for her reply, his eyes smug.

"Yeah, I guess you will," said Candy.

The smugness turned to fury as he realized his bluff had been called. "Fine," he said. He held out his hand. "Keys."

Candy handed them over.

Cy and Violet accompanied her as she walked away. When they were out of Derrick's earshot, Cy handed Candy a packet of tissues. "Thanks," said Candy as she blew her nose.

"You can borrow my bike until you get your car back."

Candy let out a laugh. "That's nice of you. Is it at your house?"

"No, it's at Riverbend Park."

"What's it doing there?"

"Long story. We'll walk you there."

"On the way," said Violet, "you could tell us more about what's going on, why someone's attacking you. We could help."

Cy looked over at Violet in surprise.

Candy shook her head. "I wish you could, but unless you can get the sheriff's department to take me seriously—"

"No, I mean..." Violet halted and faced her. "*I* want to help you. And I have literally nothing else to do."

Candy's eyebrows rose dubiously. "Really. Nothing else. You have *nothing* going on, no life of your own."

With gravity, Violet nodded. "That's essentially correct."

"She's not kidding," put in Cy. "At least not until we get results from the ad we just placed in the *Chronicle*."

Candy looked from one to the other of them. "Okay, now I'm curious."

"I'll explain my problem if you explain yours," said Violet.

"Deal."

As they headed onward, Candy's fingertips happened to brush the back of Violet's hand, and she felt an electric charge.

* * *

"Last month, Veil's Chamber of Commerce commissioned a documentary for the town's official website, to 'promote tourism and encourage residential growth.' One segment of the documentary is going to focus on our religious communities. They've already set up meetings with the reverends and the rabbi, and even though we don't have a mosque, they're talking with the one or two Muslim families that live here—which I have to give them credit for. But they draw the line at Paganism. When I told them the Wiccan community ought to receive equal representation, they told me covens don't count as organized religious groups, and they don't want to feature something 'controversial.' I've been fighting to get them to recognize us as a legitimate spiritual group. I've met with lawmakers, I started a petition—"

"A petition?" said Cy. "I'll sign."

"Are you over twenty-one?"

"N-no."

Candy turned to Violet. "Are you?"

"Um, probably, but I can't prove it."

"You really can't remember *anything* about your past?" Candy sounded fascinated.

"Nope."

"But you remember how to use chopsticks."

Violet looked down and found herself holding some noodles from her lo mein between two wooden sticks. "Apparently I do."

They were in a small restaurant called Oriental Cookery.

18

Bamboo paintings of the twelve animals of the Chinese zodiac dominated the walls.

"So when did the attacks start?" Cy asked Candy.

"A week after I went public with what I was trying to do. Someone left a voodoo doll of me at the veterinary clinic where I work."

"A *voodoo doll?*"

"It was a pretty impressive likeness. Had a pin stuck in the middle, which just goes to show how ignorant people are— voodoo dolls were originally intended for *healing* purposes. They were medicinal, not destructive. It's basically cultural appropriation... She said while sitting in a Chinese restaurant," she added ironically.

Cy gaped at her. "I'm impressed *that's* what bothers you more."

"Thank you. Anyway, back then, both the sheriff's department and the *Chronicle* took me seriously. At the time, they suspected Gabe Osher, my ex-boyfriend who got a little bit stalker-y—not as bad as your Rob, it sounds like, but still."

If either Candy or Cy noticed the flash of what might have been disappointment in Violet's eyes at the mention of an ex-boyfriend, they gave no sign.

"But after the next attack, they clearly thought I was crying wolf—the newspaper nearly said as much. I was there today because I wanted them to tell me what they're going to write about this latest incident. Well, incidents," she corrected herself.

"What exactly happened last night?" asked Violet.

"I looked behind me and there was a shadow on the wall just outside my bedroom. I slammed the door, shouted for help, called the cops, and then I heard my mother knocking on my door. Whoever it was had gotten out without her seeing them. And yes, I live with my mother. I don't have my own place yet."

"Hey, no judgment. So do I," said Cy.

Violet asked, "Could you tell if it was a man or a woman?"

Candy shook her head. "They were wearing a mask. A demon with horns, it looked like."

"And are demons something you believe in as a Wiccan?" asked Cy.

Patiently Candy said, "No, but when someone invades your home, whatever species they are, you tend to assume their intentions are hostile."

"Right, sorry," stammered Cy, flustered. "I just meant, maybe they meant to scare you the same way as with the voodoo doll. Because they assumed you *do* believe in it."

Candy nodded slowly. "You might be onto something."

"Do you suspect anyone in particular?" asked Violet.

Candy glanced around and lowered her voice. "I don't have *any* evidence whatsoever. If it comes out that I'm spreading rumors, they could claim slander and I'll lose public sympathy for my cause. I haven't even told the other witches in my coven."

"We won't tell anyone," Cy promised.

"I don't *know* anyone," Violet remarked.

Her levity made Candy smile. Then, lowering her voice further still, she said, "There are three particularly vocal opponents to my cause whom I suspect. First off, there's Bethany Williams."

* * *

"Hello! Welcome to the Veil Historical Museum. Would you like a free tour?"

"No...no thanks, I'm just going to look around. Uh, um..."

"Yes?"

"Do I...look familiar to you at all?"

"N-no, I don't think we've met."

"No, I know we haven't met, I just... Never mind."

"O-kay."

"All right, I know this sounds crazy, but...I have amnesia. I don't have a clue who I am."

"Oh... Oh! That's right, you're the one they're asking about in the paper."

"Right. It's just, I woke up today and had this feeling, this gut feeling, that I should come here. It was like...I don't know, like a sign or a message..."

"A sign from God?"

"Yeah, exactly. I don't know if you believe in that sort of thing, but that's just what it felt like. So here I am. I wondered if maybe I'm supposed to meet some person, or maybe I'm supposed to see an old photo of someone who looks like me. Maybe that person'll turn out to be my ancestor, and it'll help me discover who I am. Anyway, I'm talking your ear off, and I'm sorry for taking up so much of your time."

"No, no! It's all right. And who knows, maybe you are *here to meet someone... Hi. I'm Bethany Williams."*

"Hi, Bethany. I'm Violet."

* * *

"Bethany is the local devout Christian. She got her college degree early, like me, and became the youngest person ever to serve on one of Veil's church councils. She's literally Veil's poster child, so if she's against something to do with the town, whatever it is usually loses."

"Have you tried talking to her?" asked Violet.

Candy nodded with a tight-lipped smile. "She said she'd consider hearing me out if I considered getting baptized."

Cy shrugged. "I would've lied and said, 'Sure.'"

Candy shook her head as she cracked open a fortune cookie.

"I'm one of those idiots who values honesty. Especially when it comes to my spiritual beliefs." She read the fortune and raised an eyebrow.

"What's it say?" Violet asked her.

"'You don't have to embrace the change, just accept it.' Hm. Maybe I got yours by mistake."

"Maybe," Violet said with a laugh.

As she ate one half of the fortune cookie, Candy held out the other half to Violet. Almost without thinking, Violet opened her mouth, and Candy put the cookie in. They smiled at each other, neither one quite realizing that neither of them was speaking.

Cy cleared her throat. "So who's the next suspect?"

Swallowing, Candy said, "Next is Rabbi Metz."

* * *

"Excuse me, are you Rabbi Metz?"

"Yes, that's me!"

"Hi. I'm sorry to disturb your lunch. I'm...um..."

"It's okay, I know who you are. I'm friends with Keith—the sheriff. You go by Nelly, right?"

"Actually I'm going by Violet. May I?"

"Please. What's on your mind, Violet?"

* * *

"You see," said Candy, "these people aren't afraid I'm going to win. They don't think my petition is going to get enough signatures, or that the County Council would go along with me even if I did. But they have been complaining that I'm poisoning the town, creating divisiveness between those who support my cause and those who don't. *That's* why they might be trying to scare me into stopping—at least in the case of the first two."

"But not the third?" asked Violet.

Candy sighed heavily. "The third is Matt Foley."

* * *

II

"Excuse me, Mr. Foley?"

"What?"

"My manager asked me to catch you before you left the building. I'm supposed to remind you that your gym membership expires next week."

"Go ahead and extend me another month."

"Uh, to do that, I need a new deposit, and your credit card's expired."

"Just go ahead and extend me. I'll take care of it next week."

"But, sir, I can't, I'm not supposed to—wait, sir!"

"I said I'll take care of it! Dumbass. You gonna get out of my way, kid?"

"Matt Foley?"

"Who are you?"

"My name's Cyanne Grogan. Can I talk to you?"

* * *

"Matt Foley is a recluse who only comes out of his shell when he's pissed about something. He has no friends and never gets involved in any local events. He's apparently some kind of mathematical genius who made enough money to retire early. He doesn't need or want anything from anyone."

"Then why is he opposing you?" asked Violet.

Candy shrugged. "Because he can. He's always been openly opposed to religion, but no matter how much he complains, there's nothing he can do to shut down Jewish and Christian functions in the area. But Wiccans? A structurally disorganized group with no financially or politically powerful backers? He's spotted what he thinks of as the weak animal in the herd, and he's coming after it."

"Just out of spite?!"

"What else does he have?"

Cy had been staring off into space for a minute. Now she snapped her fingers. "I have an idea," she said. To Violet she added, "It's a little like what we did yesterday, when we exposed the kidnapper."

"Wait, that was you two?" Candy gave Violet a teasing smile. "For someone who has nothing to do, you've done a lot since you arrived."

"Candy," said Cy, "are you and the other witches in town planning on doing a ritual around Halloween?"

"The Samhain sabbat, yes," said Candy. "It's this Friday."

"I think we can use the ritual to expose who's stalking you," said Cy. "Only…somehow we need to get the three suspects to show up there."

Candy's eyebrows went up high. "Oh…"

"Maybe I can help with that," said Violet thoughtfully.

III

Bethany was the most beautiful person Violet had met in Veil, but her beauty was somehow glaring, difficult to look at. Her brown hair was long and lush, her eyes bright green, her cheeks lightly freckled, her teeth whiter than snow and perfectly straight. Despite Candy's coaching, Violet had doubted Bethany would take the bait, but it had been astonishingly easy. The devout Christian was now taking Violet on a tour of the small museum, convinced, it seemed, that Violet had been sent by God for her to assist. If that were true, the next part of the plan should go just as smoothly.

"This is a photograph of Torrance Lammwych and Johnson Thorne," said Bethany, "back when they were still friends."

Violet paused. "Lammwych... Someone said that name to me recently."

"I'm not surprised. He had a big impact on the town."

"I have to admit," said Violet, "I'm surprised to see someone as young as you so enthusiastic about history."

"Oh, no, I love it," Bethany gushed. "I majored in history in college before I moved back here. And there's always more to learn, more mysteries to solve. Take Thorne and Lammwych— did they really have a falling-out, or were they enemies all along, just *pretending* to be friends? No one knows for sure."

Just up ahead, Violet saw they were about to enter the room with the exhibit on Veil's first school. This was it: Candy had explained about how the school's history tied in with witchcraft. It was just what she needed to steer the conversation in a particular direction.

As they approached the door, Bethany caught her arm. "That room's kind of boring," she said. "The good stuff is upstairs."

Violet tried to think of a plausible reason to protest, but she drew a blank. Shrugging, she followed Bethany to the upstairs exhibits. Perhaps Bethany was uncomfortable talking about the schoolteacher who was assaulted for illustrating connections between Pagan and Christian holidays. Perhaps she only loved the history she was comfortable with.

Violet racked her brains. She had to think of another way to segue naturally to Paganism.

Then she remembered! "There was a girl named Lammwych," she blurted out. "That was it. A girl who disappeared forty-two years ago—wasn't there?"

"Yes," said Bethany, bewildered. "Roberta Lammwych, Torrance's daughter."

"Yeah, it was really weird. Some old lady thought I was her ghost or something."

"Some locals have strange superstitions."

"Yeah. Like Pagans." Violet winced inwardly but hoped she hadn't been too blunt in the transition. "They think, around Halloween, the 'veil' between this world and the realm of the dead goes away, and spirits can cross over."

Bethany gave a faint-hearted laugh. "Interesting."

Without missing a beat, and at the same time pretending to be interested in the next exhibit up ahead, Violet said, "I'm going to a Pagan ritual this Friday."

Bethany went bug-eyed. "You're what?"

"I'm going to a Pagan ritual. Some girl named Candy invited me."

"You're…into Paganism?"

"Not really. In fact, it kind of creeps me out."

"Then why are you going?"

"Well, I know hardly anybody here in town. It might be a chance to make some friends."

Bethany cleared her throat and stepped closer. "Listen, Violet, Paganism is kind of like… It's like Scientology."

"Oh, really?"

"Yes, you see, it seems interesting on the surface, but underneath, it's just a bunch of made-up nonsense. There's nothing real or meaningful in the things Pagans do, or what they believe. I mean, I'm not saying I blame them—they've been driven away from Jesus by people who have done terrible things in His name." Violet could almost hear the capital H in the pronoun. "But all the same, I wouldn't encourage them by taking part in their… activities. Tell you what, there's a service at the Presbyterian church coming up—why don't you come with me to that? I'll introduce you to lots of new friends."

"Oh! Wow, that's really nice of you. But…"

"But what?"

"Well, the thing is, that feeling that made me come here today—I've got the same feeling about the ritual on Friday. I feel like I've just got to go."

"Oh." Bethany looked blindsided and a little troubled.

It was time for the goal shot. "Hey," said Violet, "would you come with me?"

A visible, physical jolt passed through Bethany's body, which Violet pretended not to notice. "I'd feel better if I was there with someone I knew, and you've been really kind, showing me around this place. It's like I was meant to meet you."

Bethany looked away, thinking...then put on a gracious smile. "You know what? I'd love to."

"Great! Do you have a piece of paper? I'll write down the phone number of where I'm staying."

"Sure! I'll get it for you when we finish the tour."

Violet's smile was somewhat forced as she repeated, "Great!"

* * *

Rabbi Metz was a portly, bearded man in his early fifties with a yarmulke atop his bald pate. Violet didn't feel as overwhelmed by his personality as she had with Bethany. As they talked, he spoke kindly and engagingly with her, not to swell his ego but out of genuine care and generosity of spirit—or so she felt. She found herself hoping he wasn't the culprit.

Her gambit with him was similar to the one she'd used with Bethany: express interest in attending a service with him, mention she'd be going to the sabbat, and convince him to go as her chaperone.

"Basically," she said, "I'm trying out different things to see what I like, to find out more about myself."

"I think that's a wonderful thing to do. And very brave of you," he said. "I can't imagine what it's like to be in your position, but everyone I've ever talked to who's had a major upheaval, who say they don't know what to do or that the life they've had up to now is over—I tell them to keep doing things, to keep getting involved, finding connections, discovering their passions. And it sounds like you're doing that." He gave her a friendly, encouraging smile.

"Thanks," said Violet. "Just so you know, I've also thought about attending a Presbyterian service."

28

"They have nice people there, too," the rabbi said good-naturedly. "As for my people, we're not all about converting others into our faith, but you're always welcome. Like you said, you're exploring, experimenting to see what resonates."

Violet nodded. "I'm also going to a Wiccan ritual this Friday."

Rabbi Metz blinked. His smile seemed to lose some of its essence. "Wiccan ritual?"

"Yeah, this girl named Candy invited me. She was really nice."

The rabbi glanced away for a moment. Violet expected him to inquire next about how inclined she was toward Wicca, and when she gave a neutral answer, he would dissuade her from going, just as Bethany had done.

After a minute he nodded slowly and said, "Candy Windom is an intelligent, headstrong young woman. Someday she'll make a great leader."

Taken aback, Violet wasn't sure what to say next. This wasn't part of the script she'd prepared for. Should she end the conversation here and tell Candy she didn't think the rabbi was the stalker anyway? No, she couldn't do that. The plan was to get all three suspects to the sabbat, so she had to follow through on her commitment.

She took a quick breath and decided to go with the truth, or at least part of it: "Candy mentioned you, actually."

The man's eyebrows went up fractionally. "What did she say?"

"Well, she doesn't think you like her very much."

Metz tilted his head. "We have our disagreements. But I still have plenty of respect for her."

"What do you disagree on?"

The rabbi sighed. "As a rule, I don't tell people outside my faith how to worship," he said. "That's not in my purview. With that said, I've publicly opposed Wiccan gatherings in Veil."

"Why?"

"Drugs."

Violet blinked. "Drugs?"

"I have reason to believe their gatherings involve communal drug use. It may not be a popular thing to say these days, but I think recreational drugs are morally and medically unhealthy, not to mention habit-forming. Miss Windom has her heart in the right place, but she's enabling toxic, self-destructive behavior."

He stopped there. He didn't advise Violet to steer clear of the danger, only warned her about it and let her make up her own mind. She was touched.

And she knew what to say next. "Have you told the sheriff?"

"Only informally. I don't have any proof."

"Then why don't you come with me?"

He gave a slight chuckle. "Excuse me?"

"Come to the sabbat with me, but don't tell them you're coming. Make it a surprise. We can both watch for drugs."

The rabbi made a face. "I highly doubt Miss Windom would welcome me after the things I've said."

"I have a hunch she'd be really pleased to see you there." She put on the most endearing smile she could muster.

The rabbi thought it over. "Well, why not?" he said. "I needed a topic for next week's service anyway."

Violet thanked him, told him the time and place of the sabbat, and left the café really, *really* hoping he wasn't Candy's stalker.

* * *

Matt Foley was younger than Cy had pictured him. He couldn't be much over thirty, if that. His black hair shrouded his eyes, which were narrowed in a glower. He was tall and athletic, the muscles in his chest and arms as hard as his expression.

III

"What do you want?" he drawled, his voice dripping with contempt.

Candy had warned her he'd be like this. Cy kept her cool. "Did you hear about the woman with amnesia?"

"Yeah, I heard. Sounds fake."

"It's not fake. My mom offered to have her come stay with us."

"Then you and your mom are gullible." He started to swagger off.

"I heard you're opposed to the Wiccans being mentioned in the Veil documentary."

He stopped. "What's that got to do with it?"

"Violet—the woman with amnesia—bumped into Candy Windom the other day. They got to talking, and Candy invited her to this creepy ritual thing on Friday. I'm worried she's going to turn Violet into a witch."

Foley snorted. "What do you care?"

"Because then I'll have a witch living in my house! I was wondering if you could talk to Violet, convince her not to go."

"Hm… No."

Again Foley started to walk away.

He doesn't do favors, Candy had told her. *He never gives, only takes. And that's what he assumes of other people, too.*

"Fine," said Cy, apparently giving up. "Hopefully one of the other two will convince her."

Foley stopped again. "Other two?"

"Bethany Williams and Rabbi Metz. They're both going to the sabbat to try and get Violet to join their congregations." There was a particular word Candy had told her to use. Something Foley would be unable to resist. "It'll be a kind of competition between them."

31

A light was kindled in Foley's eyes. Cy tried not to watch him too closely, lest he realize he was being manipulated. *Foley can't do any more to hurt us Wiccans than he already has,* Candy had said, *but he'd jump at the chance to make life more difficult for anyone else with a spirituality.*

"Where is this ritual?" Foley asked.

IV

The plan to expose Candy's stalker at the upcoming sabbat provided a handy distraction for the next few days as Violet waited for a response to her ad (her fingerprints had turned up no results). She, Cy, and Candy met several more times to go over the plan: at the sabbat, Violet would pretend to have a flashback, a memory of witnessing one of the attacks. Candy would encourage her to remember it in detail, thus provoking a reaction from the guilty party. "We'll do it right after the apple wishes," she told her. "Remember, the key word is, 'dolly.'"

Violet soon discovered she was an early riser. With Jen at work and Cy at school, she spent her mornings scouring the internet for missing persons reports and articles about women with incredible memories. Of course, Jen had told her the sheriff's department was looking into all these cases—and with better resources—but she felt she had little else to do.

The amnesiac was Veil's new hot topic, so Cy found herself suddenly and unexpectedly popular at her school. She was the go-to person for information on the events surrounding Violet's first appearance. Cy hadn't cared much since moving to Veil about making friends (or so she had convinced herself), but now it seemed she didn't even need to make an effort.

When Jen learned of this, she nearly cried with joy.

Cy must have noticed her mother was in a better mood overall. Thus she felt it was a good time to ask: "Do you have any sexy dresses?"

At first Jen was too taken aback to answer.

"I mean, not for a date necessarily," Cy clarified, "but, like, to get someone to notice you."

Jen stammered for a moment. "Well, don't you still have that thing you wore when Rob took you to—"

"Yeah, but it doesn't fit Violet very well."

"Oh—oh, I see, this is for Violet." Again, as had happened several times this past week, Jen flinched slightly when she heard Violet's name, and even seemed to have trouble saying it. Cy burned with curiosity, but at the moment helping her friend took precedence.

A few minutes later, Cy and Violet regarded the latter in one of Jen's outfits. "I think it works," said Cy, looking back and forth from Violet to the floor-length mirror on the front of the closet door.

"Don't you think my legs might be a little cold?"

"You can put some leggings on," Cy said with an amused grin.

"Okay." Violet fidgeted, pivoting, tugging at the loose, flowing sleeves. "Whoever I was in my past life, I have a feeling I didn't do this very much."

"Do what?"

"Get dressed up, go out with people."

Cy took her fidgeting hands. "I know this isn't your best skill, but try and forget about everything else and just focus on tonight."

"Right," said Violet, taking a deep breath. "I need to remember the plan. To help Candy."

Cy rolled her eyes. "I didn't mean that. I meant…live in the moment. Try and relax. Like, maybe you weren't planning on staying in Veil this long, but if you're gonna be stuck here, you might as well try to be happy. You like Candy and she likes you, and she's nice, so don't pass up this chance."

Violet squirmed. "What if she asks me something about myself and I don't know? I don't even know if I'm gay or bisexual or…"

Cy shrugged innocently. "She could probably help you find out."

"Not helping."

"Whatever. My money's on gay."

"Why?"

"It would explain why you don't like the song 'Maneater.'"

Violet let out a giggle, and they both broke down in a fit of laughter.

When they'd recovered, Cy said, "Are you okay heading over to Candy's on your own?"

"Sure, why?"

"There's something I gotta do. I'll catch up."

It was over an hour till the ritual, but Violet didn't mind the idea of having a little time with Candy to herself. After selecting a pair of leggings, she left.

Cy found her mother getting ready to make dinner. "Mom?"

Jen looked up. "Cy, I wanted to ask you something."

That's a coincidence, thought Cy.

"Apart from last Friday and Saturday, what were the dates of the other attacks on Candy Windom?"

Puzzled, Cy said, "The dates? I don't remember. You should've asked Violet before she left." Again, the flinch. If Cy had blinked, she would've missed it.

"Do you remember about when the first one happened?" asked Jen.

Cy shrugged. "I think she said it happened around the autumn equinox."

"And the next one?"

"She found the 'Death' tarot card on her windshield the morning after that big thunderstorm, whenever that was. Apparently 'Death' isn't the tarot card you want to give someone if you're trying to frighten them. The one you want to give them is 'The Tower.'"

"Uh-huh. And the one after that?"

"Well, after that was the home invasion by the person in the demon mask while she was live-streaming."

"No, before that."

"There were no others before that."

Jen paused what she was doing. "Weren't there five attacks total?"

"No, just four."

Jen looked away, mystified. "I could've sworn Derrick said there were five."

Cy wondered about the reason for these questions, but her original curiosity took over. "Mom," she said, "why are you so uncomfortable every time somebody says Violet's name?"

Jen didn't flinch this time, but she did go still for a moment. She set aside the cooking implements. Cy saw her swallow. "Violet…was the name of a girl I knew a long time ago. A friend of mine. My best friend, actually. I guess it's disorienting, hearing her name again after so many years. Especially when someone else is using it."

"Where's your friend now?"

"She died. When I was eleven."

"Oh," said Cy, abashed. "I'm sorry."

"It's okay."

Jen sighed, eyes skyward in reminiscence. "She and I spent so much time together every summer. You see, she was five years older than I, so we never saw each other in school. No one could understand how we could be such close friends with our age difference, but it didn't matter to us. And we loved the fact that we were both named after colors. Violet and Magenta. That's why I named you and Azura…"

Cy's eyes widened. "You never told me that."

Jen gave her a rueful smile. "I should have. Tell you what, while you're at the ritual, I'll dig out some photos of her, and I'll tell you more when you get back."

She went back to cooking, but Cy stayed where she was, a troubled expression on her face. Jen paused again. "What's wrong?"

Cy drew a slow breath. "Mom, is there something else you haven't told me? About Dad's death?"

Jen frowned. "Not that I can think of." When Cy continued to stare at her, she went on, "He was staying with some friends of his on the way to Toronto. The fire was caused by faulty electrical wires. He was…unlucky."

Anger flashed across Cy's face.

"Cy, what is it? What's going on?"

In a low voice, looking daggers at the ground, Cy said, "You didn't have to kick him out."

"What?"

Cy raised her eyes and her voice. "You didn't have to make him leave us. He didn't do anything wrong."

Jen shook her head in perplexity. "Cy…we separated. We couldn't keep living together."

"No, *you* separated. He didn't want to. He wanted to work things out, but you didn't give him a chance!"

"Cy—"

"If you hadn't kicked him out, he wouldn't have been at that place when it—" She broke off suddenly, unable to look her mother in the eye.

Jen's mouth dropped open. "You…you think it's my fault that he—"

Cy beelined for the door.

"Cy, wait—wait!"

* * *

The house's front door opened a minute after Violet knocked. "Yes?"

"Hi, Ms. Windom." Violet smiled at the fiftyish woman with graying, flyaway hair.

The woman looked at her slightly askance. "Hello. Can I help you?"

Violet's smile faltered. "Ms. Windom, it's me, Violet. I came over a couple times this week to see Candy."

The woman's brow creased. "What did you say your name was?"

"Violet."

"*Violent?*"

"No, *Violet.*" Violet couldn't decide whether to be amused or exasperated.

The woman gulped. "Candace is up in her room," she said, standing back and giving Violet plenty of room to maneuver around her. Violet thanked the woman politely, but she felt her eyes on her all the way up the stairs.

"I don't think your mom likes me," she said after Candy welcomed her into her room. The witch was wearing an indigo

38

robe, a golden crescent-moon necklace, and a gold and orange headband.

"What? Of course she does," Candy said as she took Violet's coat. "Wow, you look so pretty! Here, have a seat. I'm just printing out the invocations. No, my mom's really chill. That's why I'm living with her and not my father."

Violet sat on the bed and took off her hat as Candy returned to the computer. "You don't speak to him at all?"

Candy sighed. "I try, but he keeps trying to tell me that Wicca 'doesn't look good on a resumé.'"

Violet made a wry face. "I'm sure the cats and dogs you take care of have strong objections to your religious background."

Candy gave a half-hearted chuckle.

Violet let her eyes drift across the room. Next to Candy's desk was her altar, covered with herbs, pentacles, crystals, and candles of different colors. Half her bookcase was filled with literature about Pagan history and traditions, the other half with fantasy novels by J.R.R. Tolkien, Tamora Pierce, Lloyd Alexander, and others.

Violet's gaze slid to the open door, where Candy had seen the intruder's shadow a week ago. She reflected on the three people they were luring into a trap tonight. Which one of them had crept into the house, somehow without leaving any signs of forced entry, and gotten all the way to Candy's bedroom doorway? Who was trying so hard to frighten her into ceasing her attempts to win representation for Veil's Wiccan community?

Violet's heart jumped. A shadow had just then appeared on the wall outside the door. For a moment, she'd thought the shadow's head bore horns, but then Candy's mother passed by the doorway. It had been her imagination.

Beside the door, at the edge of the dresser, an unusual item caught Violet's eye. It was a circular piece of cardboard, with a smaller circle mounted onto its center. Both circles had paper pasted on one side, and the paper displayed colorful illustrations. Violet stood and pointed. "May I...?"

"Yeah, go ahead." Candy was still focused on the documents she was printing. "That's my little Wheel of the Year."

Violet picked up the wheel and examined it. On the center circle there was a purple pentacle, with one point shaded deeper than the rest. The outer circle was divided into eight segments, each with sketches of outdoor scenes from throughout the year: snow falling, flowers blossoming, a rainbow, leaves turning, and more. The smaller circle rotated so that the pentacle pointed to each one of the scenes.

"Do these represent the eight sabbats?" Violet asked as she sat back down.

"That's right. A friend made that for me."

Violet turned the pentacle to point at a black cat. "Is it true that Wiccans think of Samhain as the start of winter?"

"Well, this one does."

"But isn't December twenty-first supposed to be when winter starts?"

"You mean the solstice?"

"Right."

Candy threw an amused glance her way. "The *midwinter* solstice, when snow's already been on the ground for weeks?"

Violet smiled back. "I see your point."

"Of course, personally, I prefer Veil's local tradition where winter officially starts whenever the first...snow falls..." She trailed off, her eyes wide with concern.

It took a moment before Violet realized what Candy was

staring at. All this week Violet had been wearing the toque whenever she visited, slipping it on every time she left the Grogan house. This was the first time Candy had seen the gash on her forehead. Violet knew that although the wound had started to heal, it still looked ghastly.

"Oh my god." Candy sat next to Violet on the bed. "What happened?"

Violet looked at the floor. This was exactly what she'd been afraid of. "I don't know," she said quietly. "It's one of the things I don't remember."

Candy's hand appeared and squeezed her knee. "That must be frustrating."

Violet looked at her, saw not pity but empathy and comfort in Candy's eyes. Her soft brown eyes.

She whispered, "It's more than that. I don't remember anything about my life. Anything I've done. I could be a horrible person and not remember it."

Candy's hand rose to Violet's shoulder. It was warm and soft.

Violet went on, wishing she wouldn't, "I just think you should know...the person you've gotten to know, the person sitting here...might not be the real me."

To her surprise, Candy smiled. "Let me tell you something," she said. "You know *The Wizard of Oz*?"

Once again Violet experienced the strange paradox of remembering a movie while being unable to remember having *seen* the movie. "Yes."

"What's the first thing Glinda says to Dorothy when they meet?"

Of course Violet knew the answer. "'Are you a good witch or a bad witch?'"

"Mm-hm," said Candy. "I love that story, but it really

frustrates me when I tell people I'm a witch, and that's the first question they ask, jokingly or otherwise. In fact, I'm not sure which is worse, the people who say witches don't exist or the ones who are so afraid of us, afraid of our 'powers,' that they have to categorize us, to decide whether they can accept us or not. We are just as human as the rest of you; that makes us good and evil mixed together, not one or the other. And just like you, we have the right to live and exist—with or without acceptance." She shook her head, her jaw tightening. "I had a teacher once who tried to get my classmates to stop using swear words. He told us if we were going to say the F-word, to replace it with 'fumble.' To replace 'shit' with 'shin guards.' And 'bitch' with..."

Violet closed her eyes and groaned.

"He gave me detention when I told him he was reinforcing a negative stereotype. But my point is," she moved her hand around to Violet's back, "we have to work harder to remember that we aren't what people fear we are. We aren't someone to be judged on sight. Everyone is entitled to the benefit of the doubt. Including you."

Her hand rose again. Violet felt her fingertips on the back of her head, gently pulling her forward. Candy leaned in, and Violet felt the brush of her lips on the wound, felt her hot breath on her forehead. With a sudden intake of breath, Violet reached up, grasped Candy's cheek and kissed her full on the mouth. Candy kissed her back, both her hands reaching around to pull Violet closer.

It was fortunate the sabbat was nearly an hour away.

V

Cy stopped at the village square to clear her head before heading on to the ritual. Truth be told, her thoughts didn't really feel that much clearer by the time she arrived, but she did feel calmer. She hadn't realized what a burden it had been, having those feelings all those months and not expressing them. Now that she had, she felt lighter. There was much more she needed to say to her mother, but it was a start.

As she approached Candy's house, Cy saw a strikingly beautiful young woman standing before it, looking uncertainly between this house and the one next door. From Candy's description, Cy guessed the woman was Bethany Williams. "It's this house," Cy told her. "If you're here for the sabbat."

"Oh, thank you." As they neared the walk leading to the front steps, Bethany hesitated, as if reluctant to let Cy get close to her.

"After you," Cy said politely.

Bethany gave her a nervous smile and went ahead. She hesitated again when they reached the porch. Cy had to circle around her to ring the doorbell.

"Are you, um," Bethany cleared her throat, "one of the... Pagans?"

"Actually I'm an atheist."

Bethany looked undecided as to whether this answer made her more comfortable or less.

Cy found a note taped above the doorbell, directing sabbat attendees to come around the side of the house. Before they could start that way, the front door opened and Candy, herself, emerged.

Bethany appeared to brace herself. "Candy…"

Before she could get further, Candy gave an audible sigh. It was not a sigh of frustration or annoyance but rather contentment. "Nice to see you, Bethany." The way she spoke, it sounded as if there were no one else in the world she'd rather see.

Cy looked at her slightly askance.

"You—you were expecting me?" Bethany stammered.

"Violet told me you were coming. She arrived early by mistake."

The plan did involve Candy acting pleased to see the three suspects at her house, but Cy thought she was overdoing it a little. The smile on her face between her rosy cheeks could be mistaken for one of genuine joy.

"Oh," said Bethany in reply. "Well, that explains why she wasn't waiting for me out front like we arranged. I almost went to the wrong house. Your neighbor's mailbox…"

"Yes, we're 42, they're 42A, it's very confusing. You can't even see the A clearly on their mailbox so we get each other's mail sometimes. One time they even found a dead bat in their mailbox." She paused. "I don't know why I said that. Sorry, I'm rambling. I do that when I'm in a good mood."

"Yes, you are," Cy murmured, her face brightening with realization.

Candy led them around the side of the house. A thick hedge divided this property from the one next door, forming a grassy alley. Just as they entered the alley, a car pulled up to the curb. "Rabbi Metz!" Candy greeted him as he got out. "What a surprise."

The rabbi gave Candy a tentative smile as he approached. "Hello, Candy. Unless you have any objection, I'm here to attend your ritual."

"Of course! You're totally welcome here. Do you know Bethany Williams?"

Taken aback by the warm welcome, the rabbi said, "Yes, I do. Hello, Bethany."

"Hello." Bethany looked bewildered and slightly wary.

Candy led the three of them along the alley to the back corner of the house, then had them halt. Around the corner were voices, most of them female, laughing and talking. Candy waved to another young woman, who approached holding what looked to be an eagle's feather and a glass phial containing burning incense. "Now, I'm glad I got the three of you at once, since I take it none of you has attended a Wiccan sabbat. Before you enter the sacred circle—or rectangle, technically, given the shape of our backyard—you have to be smudged."

"Smudged?"

Cy fought not to snort with laughter at Bethany's expression.

"It's a common practice among eastern traditions, as well as Pagan ones," the rabbi explained. "Burning sage is considered a way of purifying negative energy. Even some Christian religions still do it."

"That's right," said Candy, demonstrating as the woman used the feather to waft the fumes up and around Candy's body. "Think of it as spiritual decontamination. If you want to use the bathroom first, you're welcome to. Just remember, if you leave the circle, you'll have to get smudged again before you come back in."

The offer to use the facilities was declined, and Cy took her turn being "smudged."

"I'm really glad you're here, rabbi," said Candy before she disappeared around the corner. "There's someone I want to introduce you to. I'll go find her."

Cy followed her a minute later, and then it was Metz's turn. As he inhaled the scent of sage, he saw the look of trepidation on Bethany's face. "Bethany, it's harmless," he told her. "I promise it doesn't break any commandments."

"Maybe none of yours," Bethany muttered.

Just then a tall figure strode past her. "Hey! Stop!" cried the young woman doing the smudging. "You can't go back there. What are you doing here?"

Matt Foley sneered at her. "Relax. I was invited."

"Well—you still have to wait until I smudge you."

"Until you *what?*"

"I have to purify your energy. I just got done with the rabbi, now it's her turn, and then I'll—"

Foley ignored her and started to march on by.

She caught up to him, interposed herself and held up a hand. "No! If you go back there without our consent, you'll be considered a trespasser and we'll call the cops on you. I'm serious, Matt."

Foley stared down his nose at her. "Move it, Marcy," he growled.

A calm, deep voice said, "Why don't *I* take over the smudging?" Rabbi Metz stepped to the young woman's side and, keeping his eyes locked on Foley's, held out his hands.

V

"Whatever." The young woman handed off the sage and feather, and briskly rounded the corner of the house.

Without breaking his stare, Metz stepped up to Foley. "If you don't mind, I'll start with your back."

* * *

Two tables were set up in the backyard. One long, narrow table, set against the house, contained some light refreshments. The other was circular, laden with a curious array of objects: stones, crystals, corn stalks, incenses, oils, different-colored candles, a lighter, a bell, salt, wood chips, autumn leaves, chrysanthemums, a pitcher of water, gourds, apples, brownies (with a note marking the food as ritual equipment, not to be eaten beforehand), some small cauldrons, cloth pouches, markers, sandpaper, the documents Candy had printed earlier, and two shovels leaning against the side.

Cy eyed the table's multitudinous contents with curiosity. On the other side, Bethany eyed them with dismay. There were about a dozen other people socializing, some dressed in loose, flowing outfits like Violet's, others dressed more casually like Cy. Bethany and the rabbi were the only ones dressed somewhat formally.

One of the witches offered Bethany a drink, saying it was cider. "No, thanks," said Bethany. "I don't drink."

The witch gave her a quizzical look. "This is a Samhain ritual," she said. "We're not having alcohol."

"Oh." Bemused, Bethany accepted the drink.

"Rabbi," said Candy, drawing him aside, "I want you to meet someone." She tapped an older woman on the shoulder. "Rabbi Metz, this is Regina."

"Hello," said Regina.

"Nice to meet you."

"Well, I'll leave you guys to it." Candy abruptly departed, grinning impishly.

As the rabbi stared after her, Regina asked him, "Any idea why she wanted us to get acquainted?"

"Not a clue. Well, are you a Veil native?"

"No, I'm from Montpelier."

"And what do you do?"

"I'm a drug and alcohol abuse counselor."

"Really," said the rabbi after a momentary pause.

As Violet came out of the house through the back door, the smudging witch hurried forward with the feather and the sage. Cy sidled up to Violet when the process was finished. "So what've you been up to?" she asked with an innocent grin.

Violet grinned back and blushed. "Shut up," she whispered.

Across the yard, Candy flashed her a smile. Then suddenly something blotted out Violet's view. "You must be the amnesiac," said Matt Foley with his mouth full. In his hand was a half-eaten apple from the ritual table.

Violet stepped back, startled. Before she could reply, Bethany appeared on her other side. "Her name is Violet," she said, giving him a cold stare.

Foley snorted. "The Christian to the rescue. You like playing the 'good Samaritan,' huh?" He swallowed. "What is a Samaritan anyway?" When no one answered him, he said, "No, I'm serious. I mean, these days, who the hell knows?"

Bethany started, "The Samaritans were—"

"No, I don't mean you, you're an obsessive freak. I mean normal people. Most people nowadays think a 'good Samaritan' is just someone who does something nice. The Samaritans were people the Christians viewed as amoral. *That* was the message of the story, that the only person who did the right thing was the one person expected *not* to. If you don't know that, you miss the point." He took another bite of the apple and tossed the rest on the ground. "If you really want people to get the point of the story, you should rename it… Why not call it, 'The Good Christian'?"

He smirked at Bethany's look of hurt and outrage, but before she could respond, another voice broke in: "Because it's not specific enough. How about, 'The Good Heterosexual Cisgender White Male?'" The speaker stepped in front of him and extended her hand. "Hi, I'm Candy. Nice to meet you face-to-face."

Foley looked at her closely. "Don't I know you from somewhere?"

Candy tilted her head. "Apart from words we've exchanged online, I don't think so."

"No, I've seen you somewhere… The vet! I saw you at the vet's office last Saturday morning, when I took my dog in."

Cy and Violet looked at each other, knowing they were thinking the same thing: if Matt Foley's whereabouts were accounted for on Saturday morning, then it couldn't have been he who rigged Candy's car at the newspaper office.

Candy replied, "I wasn't at work last Saturday, but I am a vet tech, so you've probably seen me there at some point."

Foley made a face. "A vet tech? How does that work?"

"What do you mean?"

"Well, first of all, they probably have to screen you to make sure you're not stealing organs from your patients."

Candy kept her smile frozen. "You clearly know more about Samaritans than you do about Wiccans."

"Second, you could only become a vet by learning veterinary science. But you Pagans are just as anti-science as Christians."

He jerked his head at Bethany.

As Violet looked on in growing awe of her restraint, Candy folded her arms and looked politely interested. "Why do you say that?"

"Come on. The basis of any religion is belief in things that science has proven don't exist."

"There's a difference between proving something doesn't exist and not having proof that something exists. When it comes to making decisions that affect other people and the Earth, it's important that those decisions be informed by science. But when it comes to my own spirituality, my personal journey, I rely on my own experiences, which tell me of the existence of things science hasn't discovered yet."

The chatter in the area had quieted. Some stares of admiration were directed Candy's way. Even from Bethany.

"And just what experiences are those?" Foley scoffed.

"Those are private to me."

"How convenient."

"I'm not looking to beat you, Matt," said Candy. "I don't think anyone is, besides yourself. Now, I'm happy to have you join us for the ritual, but if you do something hurtful to another one of my guests, verbally or otherwise, I will have to ask you to leave."

Foley gave an incredulous laugh. "You'd kick me out? Me, but not them?" He gestured to Bethany and the rabbi.

Candy shrugged. "They seem to know how to behave themselves."

Plus, we still need to find out which of them is the stalker, thought Violet.

Foley stepped close to Candy. "They *hate* you," he said quietly. "You know they do. *I* just think you're a delusional parasite, but they are terrified of you and your witch friends. They'd be happy to see you dead."

Candy drew in a deep breath through her nose. "Maybe. But they haven't been rude."

Foley sniffed, turned on his heel, and strode off around the house, shaking his head in disgust. "All the religious nuts against the atheist," he called over his shoulder.

"*I'm* an atheist, you dick," Cy returned.

Once he was gone, chatter gradually began to spread again. "Damn, Candy," complimented Regina, to which Candy gave a small mock bow.

"I don't think I could ever face down someone in public like that," said Violet.

"I…I've had to deal with people like that before," Bethany remarked. "It never occurred to me that you would, too. Your responses are much more graceful than mine tend to be."

Candy seemed touched by the unexpected praise. "I've had a lot of practice," she said modestly. "Just not usually in person."

"Excuse me."

They turned and, to their surprise, found a newcomer standing there, someone Cy and Violet had met before.

"Kelly Upshaw, *Veil Chronicle*," she introduced herself, addressing Candy. "Your mother said the event was happening back here. Don't worry, I've been 'smudged.' Would you mind if I stayed and observed?"

Candy's demeanor toward Ms. Upshaw was blatantly icier than it had been toward Foley. "That depends," she said. "Are you planning to just observe or also participate?"

"Can I stay if I don't participate?"

"No."

"Then I'll participate."

Bethany turned to Candy. "If I participate, I'm going to need to ask what all you're planning to have us do and what all of that is for." She pointed at the ritual table.

"Sure, of course," said Candy, leading Bethany in that direction. "Let's get you a program."

"Also, why is alcohol not allowed at Samhain?"

"Well, I wouldn't say it's not allowed, but it's not a good idea when you're gonna contact the dead. After all, it's a solemn occasion."

"Whoa, hold on. When you say, contact the dead…"

They moved out of earshot. Ms. Upshaw bent her head conspiratorially toward Cy and Violet. "I got here just in time for the fireworks with Foley. Has anything else exciting happened?"

"Is that why you're here?" asked Cy. "Because of him, Bethany, and the rabbi coming to the ritual?"

"Are you kidding? Those three have made it clear they consider these…people to be at best an embarrassment to Veil, and tonight they all show up at some freaky ceremony? Something interesting is definitely going on."

Violet found herself liking the reporter less and less.

"Personally," Ms. Upshaw went on, "I'm surprised Miss Windom decided to go ahead with this event tonight. If it were me, after five attacks by an unknown stalker, I would've—"

"Four," Violet corrected her. "There've been four attacks."

Ms. Upshaw glanced toward the house. "I was told there were five."

"Nope. Four." Violet moved off to join Candy.

Not keen on being alone with the reporter, Cy started to follow.

"Hey, by the way, have you seen Rob Mulroy lately?"

Cy turned back. "Excuse me?"

"He hasn't shown up for work, and no one's seen him since last Friday."

Cy slowly shook her head. "I haven't seen him either."

Ms. Upshaw shrugged and headed toward the refreshment table, leaving Cy frowning to herself.

* * *

RELIGIOUS CEASE-FIRE by Kelly Upshaw, Veil Chronicle

A Christian, a Jew, and an atheist walk into a Pagan ritual. It sounds like the beginning of a bad joke, but this is in fact what happened last Friday night, here in Veil.

For weeks, many have been following the ongoing drama surrounding the controversy sparked by nineteen-year-old Wiccan activist Candace "Candy" Windom. Windom's outspoken desire to see Veil's Pagan community receive a mention in the forthcoming village documentary has been vociferously protested by several well-known local personalities, including Rabbi Isaac Metz, Bethany Williams of the Presbyterian Church, and mathematician Matt Foley. It was therefore a surprise to many when all three of them turned up at Windom's home to join a large group of Wiccans in celebrating the Pagan holiday Samhain (pronounced Sow-an). Even more surprising was the incident that brought the celebration to an abrupt and premature halt, followed soon after by Metz and Williams's announcement that they would both be reversing their positions and endorsing Windom's movement.

It is unclear at this point who or what induced these three outsiders to attend a ritual held by the very group they have been trying to obstruct. Metz and Williams denied having coordinated their attendance ahead of time (Foley was unavailable for comment). They both stated an expectation that they might be turned away on arrival, but they were welcomed without protest. Foley was asked to leave during the reception prior to the ceremony due to his verbal assault on one of the participants.

Williams said the ceremony was far more structured than she'd expected. It began with Windom, acting as High Priestess, reading aloud an affirmation to honor loved ones who have passed on (Williams believed at the time that the words were taken from a text, but it has since been established that all readings were written by Windom, herself, expressly for this ritual). This was followed by what is called an invocation. One of the volunteers for this activity was sixteen-year-old Cyanne Grogan, self-proclaimed atheist and friend of Windom's. "A lot of people think [Pagans] summon demons and worship Satan," said Grogan, "but those are Christian ideas. [Pagans] have their own set of deities."

What transpired over the next half-hour was a series of activities that, according to Metz, followed a set of themes: "Everything was symbolic of accepting change. Loss and gain. Mourning and celebration. Letting go of the old and welcoming the new. Viewing death with familiarity instead of fear." One such activity involved each attendee cutting an apple in half, then, aloud or privately, speaking a wish "into" the apple. They would then bury half of the apple, "planting" the wishes so they might grow to fruition. A newcomer to Wicca, Violet (who declined to give a surname), made a wish to remember more of her past.

During the next activity, corn dollies were mentioned. The word "dolly" seemed to trigger a memory flash for Violet, which she found disturbing. She described a vision of someone holding a home-crafted doll whose appearance matched the physical appearance of Windom. Windom became unnerved by this declaration, given that such a "voodoo doll" had been left for her to find at her place of work some weeks ago, with a pin stuck in its chest. Upon investigation, the sheriff's department came to suspect Gabe Osher, ex-boyfriend of Windom, though they could not prove it.

At the ceremony, Windom broke from her program to press Violet into remembering whom she had seen in possession of the doll. Violet seemed just on the point of remembering when a voice said, "It was me."

A man entered the backyard area, wearing a horned demon costume mask and wielding a knife. Many of the attendees panicked, but Windom ordered everyone to remain calm. Addressing the intruder, she asked what he wanted. He stated that he was her "horned god," here to collect the souls of everyone present. Windom declared him ignorant and ridiculous, and professed that he would be unable to harm anyone within the "sacred circle."

The intruder moved as if to attack, but was just then tackled and subdued by another new arrival: Sheriff's Deputy Magenta "Jen" Grogan, also, coincidentally, the mother of Cyanne Grogan. Deputy Grogan was pursuing a new lead discovered that day by the sheriff's department and had followed the suspect to Windom's residence.

Grogan unmasked the assailant as Gabe Osher and arrested him. He is currently in the custody of the sheriff's department.

VI

Once Gabe Osher was secure in the back of the patrol car, Jen tapped the roof to signal the driver to take him to the station. She watched until the car was out of sight, then turned back toward the house and found Cy standing there. "Hi," Jen said after a moment's hesitation.

Cy gave a small wave.

"So," Jen said awkwardly, "the reason I was asking about the dates of the attacks was that, at the station, we still suspected the ex-boyfriend, and he was in the hospital a number of nights with mono. We wanted to check if that gave him an alibi for any of the attacks, which it didn't. But then I found out something that *really* implicated him, and I figured he might try something at this ritual, so I located him and tailed him here—"

"Mom." Cy spoke quietly, not forcefully, and instantly Jen gave her her full attention. Cy glanced at her feet. "Just before Gabe showed up, we were doing this thing with apples..." She made a face, shook her head, and started over. "We were telling each other our wishes. Things we want to change... I said that I'd just had a fight with my mom, and I said something to her I didn't mean. Something really hurtful. I've been saying it to myself for months because I was angry, but it wasn't until I said it out loud that I realized I didn't really believe it. But I'd already said it to her. And my wish was that I could take it back." Her voice caught. Tears ran down her cheeks.

Jen caught her and held her. "It's okay," she whispered.

"I'm sorry, Mom. I just hate that he's gone."

"I know. It's okay."

Cy had given her tissue packet to Candy, so she had nothing with which to wipe her eyes or her nose except her sleeves. Jen suggested she go inside and find some Kleenex, and then they could talk some more. All of the other sabbat attendees except Violet had departed. The house was quiet.

"By the way," said Cy just before going in, "thanks for…you know."

"For what?"

"For getting Rob to leave town. I know I should've told you he was… Well, thanks for not making a big deal about it."

Jen stared at Cy. "Don't mention it," she said after a moment. "Go on in. I'm going to make sure they got Gabe Osher to the station." She took out her cell phone as Cy went into the house. She dialed a number. "Benno? It's me. I need a favor. I need you to find someone. Rob Mulroy."

* * *

"All this time I thought someone was coming after me because I'm fighting for what's right. But all along it was just about some dumb boy's entitlement."

Violet had been helping Candy bring food and dishes in from the backyard. Now they stood in the kitchen together, taking a break. "At least Bethany and the rabbi are supporting you now," said Violet.

Candy looked ill at the mention of Bethany. "Before she left, Veil's poster child told me she understands now—that Wiccans are really Christians even though they don't know it, 'worshipping God in their own way.' She compared us to people reading *The Chronicles of Narnia* and not knowing the lion Aslan is really Jesus."

"Oh. W-well, maybe if she comes to more sabbats, she'll eventually figure it out."

Candy shook her head. "I'm not crazy about seeing more of her." She stepped forward and circled her hands around Violet's waist. "The question is, will I be seeing more of you?"

Violet blushed. "Well, I guess, as long as I'm stuck here," she teased, reaching around Candy's neck. "I assume you're not going anywhere."

"You bet I'm not."

They kissed just as Cy walked into the kitchen, drying her eyes. Smoothly she did an about-face and walked right back out.

Giggling, Candy said, "It's all right, Cy."

From outside the door, Cy called, "You sure? 'Cause Mom and I could just leave."

"You tell your mom she's officially my favorite deputy."

Violet stroked Candy's hair. "I could stay and, you know... keep helping you and your mom clean up."

Candy hugged her. "Thanks. I think Mom needs the house to just herself and me tonight. But I'll call you tomorrow."

Violet left Candy's house thinking that, in spite of the confrontation with the knife-wielding Gabe, this was the best day she'd had since she woke up in Veil. And the days only looked to get better.

"So," Cy said to her mother as the three of them headed toward the car, where the bicycles had already been stowed, "you were saying how you figured out it was definitely Gabe who was the stalker."

"Well, I asked Deputy Derrick why he thought there were five attacks instead of four, and he told me Gabe Osher was picked up for a DUI earlier this month. While he was in a holding cell, Gabe protested that he was innocent, not only of the DUI but also of putting a dead bat in the Windoms' mailbox the night before."

"Wait, what?"

"That's what I thought. I looked into the incident and found that that had happened to the Windoms' *neighbors*. Gabe had accidentally confessed to an attack that no one even knew was an attack."

"Oh my god—he got the wrong house! The first two attacks happened at Candy's car and her workplace. He must never have gone to her house while they were dating. Jeez, if Derrick had just paid a little more attention, this would've been over weeks ago and Candy wouldn't have had to—Violet?" Cy had glanced back at Candy's house and found that she and her mother were the only two still walking. Violet had halted several paces back. "Violet, are you okay?"

Violet's face was creased with shock and dismay. She pivoted, at first hesitantly, then with urgency. She marched back to Candy's front door and on inside.

In the kitchen, she found the person she sought putting the dishes away. She stood in the doorway and said in an outraged whisper, "Did you do it? Did you hire Gabe Osher to do all those things?"

Candy's mother stared back at her with a deer-in-the-headlights expression and didn't reply.

Candy, herself, entered from another door. "Violet?"

But Violet didn't take her eyes off the mother. "Did you hire Gabe Osher to terrorize your own daughter?"

The older woman's eyes flicked sideways. "Candace, I think your friend's had too much alcohol."

"Violet, what are you doing?!" cried Candy. "Of course she didn't hire Gabe!"

Cy and Jen caught up in time to hear Violet say, "Gabe meant to put the dead bat in your mailbox, but he got your neighbors by mistake." She took a step toward Candy's mother. "When Kelly Upshaw spoke to you, you told her there were *five* attacks, not four. That was a slip, wasn't it. How could you know, unless you were responsible? You *told* Gabe the address, but he couldn't tell which mailbox was y—"

"Violet, stop!" Candy took a stance between Violet and her mother. "My mother is the only one who's been supportive of me my whole life. She's the only family I have who's never judged me or been afraid of me."

But Cy was watching the older woman as Candy spoke. She saw her tremble, glimpsed repressed emotion threatening to break through. After the last four months, Cy knew something about that. She realized what was about to happen. Looking over, she saw that her own mother had realized it, too.

"There are so few people who are naturally loving and accepting," Candy went on, "and I'm lucky to have a parent who's one of them. She's my rock. If you're gonna treat her like this, then you need to le—"

"It was just supposed to be a phase!!"

Mrs. Windom avoided her daughter's eyes as her words gushed out: "You're a teenager! Teenagers do weird, stupid things because their brains aren't formed right yet and they have to experiment. Pills, tattoos, BDMS...w-witchcraft..."

Candy took a step back. "Mom??"

"But then you were supposed to grow out of it! I kept waiting and waiting. I see people in town staring—they think I'm a bad mother. But they don't understand! If I told you no, you'd just keep on doing it anyway. And if I'd tried to force you, you would've put a spell on me."

Candy's legs gave way. Violet fumbled to catch her as she sank to the floor.

"I contacted a priest and asked what I should do. He said it was too late—you're probably already possessed by a demon. He said I should kick you out of the house. But I couldn't do that because I love you." She gave her daughter a desperate, appealing look.

Candy was dumbstruck, her face pale, ashen.

"So I thought, if God gave you some warnings, you'd come back to him. I was very specific about what I told Gabe to do— just *frighten* you, never hurt you. You know, the cherry soda didn't have real cherries. You might have *thought* it could kill you, but you were never in any real danger. You just needed a little wake-up call, sweetheart." She spread her arms and moved toward Candy—and promptly found Jen blocking her way. The older woman shook her head in protest. "But you understand, don't you?" she squeaked. "You're a mother. Sometimes the only way to protect your child is to lie to her—just a little."

A tremor rippled through Jen Grogan, but she quashed it by the time she spoke. "Right now I'm not a mother. I'm a sheriff's deputy. And I'm asking you, Candy," she turned to Candy, "if you want to press charges."

With support from Violet and Cy, Candy got to her feet.

Her mother stared at her half-resentfully, half-beseechingly.

"No," said Candy hollowly. "But I am going to go upstairs and pack, and call my dad. I'm going to move in with him, if he's okay with it. If not, I'll check into a motel. Either way," she looked at Jen, "if you could get Deputy Derrick to return my car, I'd appreciate it."

"But—" As her mother reached out to her, Jen stepped closer and shot a fiery warning from her eyes.

Candy squeezed Violet's hand but didn't look at her before she went upstairs.

* * *

"Did I do the right thing?"

They were in the car, on the way home. They had stayed at Candy's house until her father arrived from a nearby town. Jen had briefly spoken to him alone. Candy had not come back downstairs before they left.

Cy, who shared the backseat with Violet, turned to her. "What do you mean? Of course you did."

"But she's heartbroken. You heard her; her mother's her rock. Or she was. I took that away from her."

"No, you didn't. Her mother was lying to her, and you exposed it."

The two of them were looking at each other, so neither one saw Jen eyeing Violet apprehensively in the rearview mirror.

Cy went on, "Even if that woman thought she was doing the right thing for her daughter, she was hurting her and needed to be stopped. You had to show Candy the truth. I mean, honestly, could you have lived with yourself if you hadn't?"

"What if she never speaks to her mother again?"

"That's up to her. And her mother should've thought of that before she did what she did. Hey, you missed a stop sign, Mom."

Epilogue

It was an hour before daybreak. Matt Foley liked to do his jogging before any other exercisers appeared (save for the occasional annoying bike-rider).

His humiliation from the night before was a thorn in his side, goading him to greater speed. When he paused at the end of the footbridge over the Greene River, as he always did, he was more out of breath than usual. His heavy breathing could be the reason he didn't hear footsteps approaching from behind.

How was he going to get back at her—humiliate that witch in return? Well, there were plenty of ways to embarrass a girl that age. He'd think of something. He was easily the smartest person in Veil, and if he devoted all his time to thinking about it—

That was when the first blow fell, cracking against his back and shattering at least two ribs. He grunted and spun around, in so doing presenting his abdomen as a target. The next blow caught him in his midsection, knocking the wind out of him to prevent him from crying out. He saw the attacker raise the stick again.

It was over in less than half a minute. Foley's attempts to defend himself were pitiful, or so thought his attacker. The last blow splintered his skull and sent him reeling over the side and off the bridge. He fell head-first into the shallows, breaking his neck on impact.

His murderer observed him from the bridge and nodded in satisfaction.

The bloody stick was left wedged in the metalwork, where it was sure to be found by anyone who came looking for it.

The murderer trotted away, whistling a tune.

WINTER IN VEIL

A Mystery Novella Series
by Miles Ledoux

Next time in Veil...

"What do you want?!" the sheriff hollered above the noise of the acetylene torch. "Why are you terrorizing these people?!"

A groan sounded from the floor nearby. The Welder slowly turned his head to regard the old woman's prone form.

"What are you doing?!" thundered the sheriff, relieved that the heat was subsiding but alarmed to see the Welder advancing toward the barely conscious woman. "You leave her alone!!"

The Welder looked up at him and tilted his head, as if to say, *Or what?*

About the Author

Miles Ledoux was born in upstate New York and started writing murder mysteries at the age of nine. His first paid writing gig was in 2007, when a local theatre chose one of his plays for their summer melodrama. He received other royalties after moving to Los Angeles for graduate school, where he wrote, directed, and produced several mystery dessert theatre plays. He also started a side business designing and running mystery party games while working as a martial arts instructor.

Currently the author resides in Springfield, Vermont. Despite having lived in five different states, he has remained active in community theatre as a playwright, director, and actor. He also has a YouTube channel where he compares Agatha Christie adaptations to the books they were based on. His handle is @MysteryMiles.

Miles loves books, cats, music, Star Trek, Peanuts, and owns an ever-growing number of variations of the board game Clue. His favorite author is Lloyd Alexander.

You can connect with me on:

🌐 https://www.ledouxmysteries.com